Dedication

Saronda Coleman-Singleton

Cynthia Marie Graham Hurd

Susie Jackson

Ethel Lee Lance

Depayne Middleton-Doctor

Clementa C. Pinckney

Tywanza Sanders

Daniel Simmons

Myra Thompson

Nine African American parishioners
gunned down during Bible Study at the
Emanuel African Methodist Episcopal Church
in Charleston, South Carolina, June 17, 2015.
Nine martyrs to racism and intolerance,
they will rest always with their Lord.

Spenser's Story of Harriet Tubman

ISBN-13: 978-1543287745 | ISBN-10: 1543287743

This book is available in both soft cover and e-book
at Amazon.com, or through our website at
www.OzymandiasPublishing.com.

Special Thanks

Over the years since Harriet Tubman lived, there has
been an enormous amount of material written about her...
for both children and adults. Much of it, for a variety of
reasons, is now thought to be inaccurate. Fortunately,
there is a recent book which presents some of the
best research yet on Harriet Tubman's life. It is:

**Bound for the Promised Land: Harriet Tubman—
Portrait of an American Hero** by Kate Clifford Larson.
One World Ballantine Books, New York, 2003.

Where material may be in dispute I have relied on
Ms. Larson's research in her book. Without her efforts
to offer readers a historically accurate portrayal of
Harriet Tubman, I would have been a lot less confident
of my facts. Of course, any factual errors or omissions
within **Spenser's Story of Harriet Tubman** are mine alone.

Thanks also to Ray Driver, illustrator; Isadora Tang,
the book's designer; Juliet Foster, our manager
and overseer; Aimee Clark and Paul Sturm,
editors extraordinaire; and Theresa Clark, who kept
me focused and did everything she could to save me
time and improve the book. She always knows what
makes the most sense.

Ozymandias

Publishing Co.

A Word from the Author

Ozymandias Publishing Co. is an independent publisher. It is not affiliated with a large, traditional publisher which must prioritize books based on the likelihood of profits.

Ozymandias Publishing Co. is unlikely to make money, and that is okay with me because its first priority is to offer readers top quality books at reasonable prices. It provides me an opportunity to reach readers—both children and adults—with an educational and entertaining product.

Independent publishing is not a product of vanity for most writers, it is more a function of independence and an itch that can only be scratched by writing. In my case I do not have the time necessary to go through the agent/publisher process, which is time-consuming. I spent my career working to support my family as best I could, and writing books for children was not how I did it.

I am not so young anymore, and I want at this point to reach children and write stories about their heritage. Although every book sold reduces my overhead, profits do not motivate me.

I write to educate and inform both children and adults. I hope that with examples like Harriet Tubman to drive them they will become involved in their communities, and try to improve society in whatever way they can.

I have written at this point only two stories by Spenser. But if given decent health and time, I hope to write a bunch more.

If you like *Spenser's Story of Harriet Tubman* please pass it along to a friend or library. Books buried unread on shelves is a painful waste. Keep Reading; Keep Learning; Never Stop.

-PsC

Editor's Preface

As I read through the remarkable journals of Spenser, which I found in an old trunk a couple of years ago, I noted Spenser's first-hand story of Harriet Tubman. As you may know if you read Spenser's earlier journal on the writing of the Constitution, he is one of the most literate and adventurous cats in American history.

Now Spenser tells the story of one of the most extraordinary and brave women in our nation's history.

Harriet Tubman could not read or write. But that was not because she did poorly in school, or skipped class. When Harriet was a child she was a slave and owned by a 'master' who did not let his slaves learn to read or write.

In fact, almost no slaves anywhere could read or write because their owners encouraged the passage of laws that prohibited slaves from going to school.

They thought that if slaves were educated they would expect more from life than being owned and mistreated like some farm animals. They feared slaves would get together and overrun and kill their owners in order to be free. Most owners forced their slaves to carry passes when they left their plantations. If the slave did not have a pass they would be returned to their owner and were often whipped.

Much of the history of slavery comes to us today through stories told by word of mouth from one generation to the next. Often these stories were not written down, and so over the years some of the stories we learn about today were wrong or exaggerated.

Unfortunately, many facts about Harriet's life, and childhood in particular, still are not known. Facebook and other social media sites did not exist then.

I have edited Spenser's story to leave out as many mistakes or unproven tales about Harriet as I could. For example, some writers/historians say that Harriet helped more than 300 slaves travel on the Underground Railroad [UGRR] to freedom. Others say that about 70 slaves were conducted by Harriet from slavery to freedom—not 300.

Spenser did not know the answer to this question, nor do I, although the true number is certainly much closer to 70. More important than numbers, however, is that this remarkable person risked her life many times to free her people from slavery.

Her heroism was not hers alone. There were many other slaves who risked their lives to escape. And others of both races who dedicated themselves to overcoming slavery—among them abolitionists [anti-slavery activists], workers on the Underground Railroad and soldiers who fought and died in the Civil War.

But this is mostly the story of one woman who would not give in to beatings and whippings that could have killed her, but which instead made her tougher and gave her the strength to overcome adversity and live life on her own terms, not those she was born into.

Spenser's Story of Harriet Tubman is the story of an American hero, an African American woman who was born into slavery but who escaped from it and then returned many times at great risk to her own life to help others.

Insights

"...there was one of two things I had a right to, liberty or death; if I could not have one I would have the other; for no man should take me alive; I should fight for my liberty as long as my strength lasted, and when the time came for me to go, the Lord would let them take me."

—*Harriet Tubman*

"...I have wrought *(worked)* in the day—you in the night. I have had the applause of the crowd and the satisfaction that comes of being approved by the multitude *(many people)*, while the most that you have done has been witnessed by a few trembling, scarred, and footsore bondmen and women *(slaves)* whom you have led out of the house of bondage, and whose heartfelt "God Bless You" has been your only reward."

Frederick Douglass

—*Letter from Frederick Douglass to Harriet Tubman, August 29, 1868*

"Children, if you are tired, keep going; if you are scared, keep going; if you are hungry, keep going; if you want to taste freedom, keep going."

—*Harriet Tubman*

"We've got to tell the unvarnished truth."

—*Historian John Hope Franklin, 2005*

The Moses of her People

№1

I had been waiting for Harriet for several hours in the rain. The water ran down my whiskers like snow melting down a mountain side.

Harriet was late—quite a bit late—and I was getting worried. It was past midnight and I had expected Harriet and her passengers to meet me much earlier.

Harriet Tubman almost always traveled by night and used the bright North Star as her guide. But this night rain clouds darkened the sky and the North Star could not easily be seen.

Nonetheless, she knew where I was waiting, we had done it several times before.

Just as I was beginning to despair of her arrival I heard the loud screech of an owl. Finally she had come. I immediately returned my best owl call in answer to signal it was safe to continue. I hoped while I waited that Harriet would know it was me—cats are not always good at making bird calls.

Then she was standing next to me along with two women, one with a baby, two young children and a tall man black as the night. They were even wetter than I was, and looked like they had been swimming in their clothes.

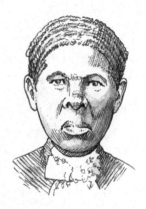

Harriet Tubman

"Spenser," said Harriet as we hugged, "we have had a difficult journey. But we can discuss that more when we are warm next to a big fire."

"Maggie has already made the fire and is waiting for us," I said. "And she has made a late meal as well. But now let's get out of this rain."

I gently urged Charley, my horse, to start and the wagon slowly moved forward along a narrow dirt path that stretched through a thick forest of dark trees. I lived in a farmhouse a little more than two miles from the woods.

It was early in January, only a few weeks after Christmas. Harriet sometimes used the holiday season or weekends to conduct her passengers north. She felt that slave owners were less watchful when their families were gathered, and perhaps had drunk a few too many beers.

Also, many local newspapers did not come out every day so a reward notice for escaped slaves which would be displayed on trees and in shops might be delayed long enough for them to get a head start.

This did not guarantee escape, but it gave conductors on the Underground Railroad a little better chance. Harriet was one of these conductors, and I was a station master.

The Underground Railroad was neither underground nor a real railroad. It was a network of people and safe places which helped slaves from the south reach safety in the north where slavery was unlawful.

Conductors like Harriet helped slaves travel to safety by guiding [conducting] them to safe locations [stations] where they could hide from slave hunters, rest and recover their strength before moving along to the next house, church or other safe house on their journey.

The farm house where I lived with my wife Maggie and eight children was sold to me by Mr. Thomas Garrett, a Quaker abolitionist who lived in Wilmington, the largest city in Delaware.

My house was on a farm outside of New Castle, a lovely little town south of Wilmington. It was set back a quarter mile from the nearest road so unexpected, unannounced visitors were rare. But we could never be sure so we kept a careful watch for slave hunters.

The reward for escaped slaves was commonly $100 for a captured slave returned to his owner, and often many times this amount. Slave hunters could make a lot of money hunting runaways.

---

* Editor's note: A $100 reward for capturing a runaway slave in 1850 would today equal $ 2,917. It's important to understand how much value a slave had for slave hunters or sellers. $100 then is much more than $100 in 2017.

Spenser's Farm

A slave returned by a bounty hunter was important to the owner because it showed other slaves they would be hunted down and returned. They would be brought back in chains. Then usually they would be beaten severely. In some cases they were beaten to death or even lynched to serve as examples to other slaves that escape could mean death.

---

* Editor's note: *Lynching* occurred when a person was hanged by a rope from a tree until dead. It continued long after slavery ended, right up through the Jim Crow era of the 20th century.

Mr. Garrett's nephew, who lived in my house before it was sold to me, wanted to live nearer to his family and church and so he moved to Wilmington. He was a station master on the Underground Railroad, and Mr. Garrett made certain that I would carry on this important work before he sold me the house.

While I am not a Quaker, I am known as a strong abolitionist, so Mr. Garrett knew I would continue his nephew's work.

---

* **Editor's note:** An 'abolitionist' was a person who believed that slavery was wrong, that people should not own or be owned by other people. They wanted to abolish slavery. Abolitionists included both black people and white people— and one cat—who lived in both the north and the south.

Now, as Charley slowly pulled his heavy load down the bumpy road, the baby sleeping in his mother's lap next to me woke up suddenly and screamed.

Harriet, standing behind us in the wagon, immediately reached into her pouch, took out some white powder and quickly put it in the baby's mouth with her thumb.

"We can't have any commotion now," she said to Bess, the young mother. "The baby needs to sleep a little longer if we are going to get to Spenser's house.

Harriet knew that babies traveling north could not be trusted to keep quiet. Babies just do what babies do—cry and scream as loud as they can when they're tired or hungry or just feel like crying.

So Harriet always gave babies a drug to keep them asleep—usually laudanum— while they were on the road. The quickest way to alert slave hunters was a screaming baby, especially in dark woods at night.

---

* Editor's note: Laudanum was used for lots of purposes, including as a pain killer and sleep aid. It was available in plantation stores, so Harriet did not need to ask a doctor for it.

Our journey otherwise was uneventful and we reached the farm as quickly as old Charley could get us there. Maggie looked relieved when she met us at the door, she always worried that something bad might happen.

While the rain had ended we were all soaked and the first thing Maggie did was to provide everyone with dry clothes. Then we removed a table and large rug that covered a hidden door in the floor. It led to a secret basement below the dining room.

Harriet and her passengers would stay in this room overnight. We could not take a chance that slave hunters would break in and find the escaped slaves, so they stayed hidden all night.

While Maggie was providing our hungry guests with food, including a recently butchered roasted pig with vegetables from our garden that she had canned in autumn, Harriet and I added logs to the fire that would keep the travelers warm. The smoke from the fireplace was masked by another fireplace and chimney directly above the hidden room.

---

* **Editor's note:** Spenser knew that Harriet and her passengers were hungry. They had been on the road for several days with only what they found or took from farms at night to eat. Typically escaped slaves ate wild nuts and berries; corn and apples from the fields; fish and rabbits if they could catch them; and farm animals like pigs and chickens if they could be taken without alerting the farmer. They could not cook anything because a fire at night aroused suspicion and brought slave hunters.

Once everyone had eaten and settled down to rest on mats near the fire Harriet explained why they were late.

"Coming up from the shore *[the Eastern Shore of Maryland]*," she said, "some slave hunters with dogs picked up our smell. Maybe one of the other slaves from around Church Creek told them we escaped.

They tracked us for miles," she said, "and almost got us a couple of times. Finally, when we got to the woods a little down the road from you, they were pretty close. We could hear the dogs barking they were so close."

The tall man shook his head, "I know for sure we not going to make it. Can't hide from those blood hounds, least not for long. I tell Harriet I die before they take me back."

Then Bess, his wife, said she sure was not going back either. "Mr. Horatio, he own us, he real mean. Evil mean. One time he whip Sam so bad he near die, then make him be in the field the next day. Only Sam be able to work all day. Anyone else dead.

"And my sister Sarah there," pointing to the younger woman, "she owned by Mister Robert. He treats slaves better. He whips her some, but not too bad."

"Amen," said the young woman barely old enough to be a mother. "Sometimes he lets Jane go with no whipping, she so young," pointing at her child.

"Then," Harriet said, "we came to that stream, the one that snakes on through the trees. But with all the rain we had it was more like a river—wider and deeper than most times. Even Sam was not willing to just walk into that river."

"I can't swim. I more scare of that water than I am of any whipping from Master Horatio," Sam said.

"Well," said Harriet, "we had to cross that water or we would be caught. So I told them all to stay put and I started across holding my pistol above my head so it would stay dry.

"That river was mighty cold and running fast," she continued. "Got hit by a couple of chunks of ice coming down, and it got deep little by little. When I was in the center that water was rushing past my ear louder than a church spiritual.

"Finally," she said, "I got across. Since I ain't too tall I figured everyone but the children could get across too. [Harriet was about five feet tall]. So I came back across. Sam took his son James on his shoulders and his baby in his arms.

"I put little Jane on my back, she held my pistol up, and the women locked arms.

---

* **Editor's note:** Harriet always carried a pistol hidden in her clothing, she said it was just in case one of her passengers got scared and wanted to turn back. She said she would threaten them with the gun—maybe even shoot them if necessary—to make them keep on moving or to protect her other passengers. But she never had to use it.

"We got mighty wet, and bad cold, but we all got across. James wanted to hold that pistol, but I wanted it nearby me, and that little Jane did just fine."

Harriet paused and the child James said in his most grown up voice, "Before we get out that water we walk a long way in the shallow water near the bank. Miss Harriet say that make it hard for the dogs to smell us, and it help us escape."

Harriet smiled at James and nodded to Sam. "The good Lord, he got us through that water, ain't nobody but Him do it. That did not mean He made us warm and dry. It sure was cold, let me tell you."

While everyone was safe and dry now and near a warm fire, Sarah and little Jane were both still shivering. It had not been an easy trip for anyone.

Harriet Talks About Growing Up a Slave

"Harriet," I said, settling down by the fire, "tell me what you remember when you were a slave growing up, if you don't mind telling."

"Not much to tell," she said.

I knew Harriet did not talk about herself much. Everything she did and believed in came from her faith. I knew that she believed God would take care of her until it was her time to go. Then He would take her home. Her faith made her as fearless as any person I ever knew.

Harriet began: "My Momma was a slave for Mr. Edward Brodess. Her name was Harriet Greene Ross and they all called her Rit. When I was a baby we moved to Mr. Edward's farm near Bucktown.

* **Editor's note:** Bucktown was outside Cambridge in Dorchester County on the Eastern Shore of Maryland.

"When I was born I was named Araminta and called Minty for short."

"When did you take the name Harriet instead of Araminta?" I interrupted.

"Oh," she said, "that was later when I married Mr. John Tubman."

I wanted to press her why she changed her name to Harriet, but she would tell me if she wanted to. She never did, although many people thought it was to show respect to her mother.

"My father's name was Ben Ross, so my name was Araminta Ross. My Daddy was a slave for Mr. Anthony Thompson, and he worked for Mr. Anthony cutting timber and then getting it hauled down the road or floated on the canal to the wharves for shipping.

* **Editor's note:** Joseph Stewart's Canal was built by both slaves and free black men between about 1810-1832. This small waterway was completed when Harriet was between 10 and 12 years old.

"When I was a little girl old Master Edward rented me to Miss Susan, who had a new baby. I was supposed to clean and dust the house every day, do some sewing and then rock the baby to sleep at night and be sure it did not cry and wake up Miss Susan. *[Harriet was likely no older than six at this time, perhaps younger]*.

"Well," said Harriet stiffening some, "that woman whipped me for not cleaning right, and I was never taught how to clean dust. Seems I left the windows closed so that dust just fell back down where it always was.

"Then one night the baby got sick and started to crying. I was so tired I fell asleep with that baby still crying. Miss Susan beat me till she broke some of my ribs. And me only barely a child myself. Finally Master Edward had to take me back.

"When I got better I worked in the corn fields, milked cows and dug taters. Almost any work to do I did. I got pretty strong and Daddy would have me drive ox teams to clean up the fields or haul timber."

"How old you then?" asked James, who I guessed to be seven or eight years old.

"Maybe seven or eight," Harriet said, looking the boy straight in the eye.

"Wow," said James, "you pretty tough."

"Course," said Harriet, "I could have been 11 or 12," smiling quickly at Sam.

The boy looked relieved, and Harriet continued. "I could cut a half-cord of wood in one day, a full cord in two. By myself."

* Editor's note: A cord of wood is four feet high, four feet wide and eight feet long.

"Master Edward's farm—it was not really big enough to be called a plantation— was near a swamp. I was told to check the muskrat traps in winter during the trapping season. And it was almost as cold and wet as crossing that stream today, you know it too."

"So you're used to wading in cold, frigid water," I suggested in a weak attempt at humor.

"You never get used to being cold," Harriet said. "Or hungry either." She was not angry at me for the comment, just remembering back to so much cold and hunger, and there was nothing funny about that.

"Then," she said, "I guess when I was a teenager—about 13 or 14—I went to the store in Bucktown to carry some supplies back for the cook. While we were in the store another slave from nearby came in without a pass or permission. His overseer [field boss] came in later and saw the slave and told me to help hold the man down."

Harriet looked pained as she remembered. "I could not do that, and the other slave tried to run away. The boss man picked up a heavy metal weight from the counter and threw it. It hit me upside my head. It broke my skull and drove part of my head wrap into my brain I imagine. My hair had never been combed and it stuck out like a bushel basket. That hair maybe saved my life.

"They carried me to the house all bleeding and fainting. I had no bed, no place to lie down on at all, so they lay me on the seat of a loom and I stayed there all that day and next.

---

* Editor's note: A loom at that time and place likely was a small, hand and foot operated machine that a person most-often used to weave thread into clothes.

Then I went back to the field and worked with the blood and sweat rolling down my face till I couldn't see."

"What happen to you is why we run away," Sam said, "and," Bess interrupted, "why we not ever go back. We never let that happen to James while we alive."

Harriet went on, "Mr. Edward tried to sell me, but no one wanted a weak, sick slave girl. They said they would not pay sixpence for me."

While Harriet eventually recovered her strength, the injury damaged her brain. Several times I had seen her have a seizure, sometimes in the middle of a sentence, or driving a horse cart or eating a meal.

---

* Editor's note: For Harriet Tubman, her seizures amounted to falling instantly and deeply asleep. A seizure could last for just a few seconds or minutes, or longer, often followed by a bad headache.

A sleeping fit at the wrong time, of course, could cost Harriet and her passengers their lives. Up to now that had not happened. We all prayed it never would.

By this time it was very late at night, and the women and children had long ago fallen asleep. Even Sam was beginning to nod off.

Harriet and I tossed several more logs on the fire so its warmth would last through the night, and I thanked her for her stories.

"We'll plan to rest for a day and another night. The women and children are exhausted and it would be good for them to rest up," Harriet said, "they still have a long journey ahead before we get to the Promised Land."

"Of course," I said, "perhaps you will continue your story again tomorrow night, maybe explain how you escaped the first time."

"I will do my best Spenser, we sure do appreciate the kindness you and Maggie have showed us," she said before she lay down and fell fast asleep.

No 3

It's All About Family

During the night no bounty hunters appeared, so in the morning I opened the secret door and said it was safe to come up to the kitchen for some breakfast. Maggie had fixed eggs, bacon, bread and butter with hot coffee for everyone and milk for the children. It did not last long, but everyone was satisfied.

Because our house was surrounded by fields and the north-south road was a quarter-mile away and anyone approaching the farm during daylight could be seen, Harriet and her passengers were safe upstairs until the sun went down.

Bess's baby was given a day without sleeping medication, and the children got a chance to play some with our children in the space behind the house. Several of them were the same age, so the time was fun for all. Certainly James and Jane deserved to play like children for a bit, not just work in the fields all day as slaves.

Bess and Sarah helped Maggie around the house, along with Nina, one of our older daughters.

When it grew dark again, everyone went back to the safe room below, and Harriet continued her story after we had finished dinner.

"First time I tried to escape," she started, "I likely was about 27 or so, maybe a little older. It was the year 1849 and Master Edward said he wanted to sell me south. I was pretty sick that year so maybe no one wanted to pay much for me until I got better.

"I prayed he would change his mind. You see, slaves who are sold south were never seen again. Never knew their families. They just disappeared like they never existed. Except we remembered them, and they remembered us, but we all knew we never were going to see each other again.

"When I was a teenager Master Edward sold my sisters Linah and Soph," continued Harriet. "I remember watching them sold while I was sitting on a fence rail. They were crying and wailing all the way down the road until they disappeared. And I remember the chains and their bloody legs when they were put up in the wagon.

"Now, it was my turn," she said. "When my prayers did not stop Master Edward from trying to sell me south,

I asked the Lord to kill him and take him out of the way. My brother Robert always said Master Edward was not fit to own a dog.

"Well, Mr. Edward up and died the next week. I then had to pray to the Lord to forgive me for those prayers, I felt mighty bad. But now Miss Eliza, Mr. Edward's widow, tried even harder to sell me. So me and my brothers Ben and Henry decided to leave before I was sold.

"We started off, and got up the road a bit," Harriet said, "when my brothers said we needed to turn around before we got caught. They were afraid we would not make it. And they made me go back with them, like I had no other choice.

"We got back so soon Miss Eliza was not really sure we were gone, she thought so but maybe did not know for sure. Or did not care 'cause we all came back. So nobody got whipped that time. Still, I know she would not change her mind about selling me, so a couple of days before she took me to the market to sell me I left again, this time just me."

When Harriet paused to take a breath little James asked, "You just left, not tell your Momma or anyone? You have any children, or a man?"

Harriet answered James directly and said, "I could not tell my mother 'cause she would get all upset and try to make me stay, and I knew the next day I would be sold down to Georgia or someplace real bad. But I told my friend Mary, who was working inside, by singing a song that told her I was leaving.

Next day she told Momma and Daddy that
I left for the north.

"I'm sorry I'm going to leave you,

Farewell, oh farewell;

But I'll meet you in the morning,

Farewell, oh farewell.

"I'll meet you in the morning,

I'm bound for the Promised Land,

On the other side of Jordan,

Bound for the Promised Land."

---

* Editor's note: This was a church spiritual. It meant Harriet
was bound for the Promised Land in the north. Tubman and
other conductors on the Underground Railroad used songs
that could mask from their oppressors what they really
meant, sometimes taken from church hymns or the Bible.

"A couple of years before this I had
married Mr. John Tubman, a free black man.
Now this did not make me free, just married,
and John argued with me not to go. But, he
would not come with me and so I left him...
and my Momma, Daddy and brothers too.
I wanted to be free, not a slave in Maryland
or Georgia."

James had another question, "How can a slave be free? Like you say Mr. John was."

"James," she said, "a black person is free if he is born up north, where we are going. When you get there you will be free too, at least once we get to the Promised Land where those slave hunters can't get you. Some others work to buy their freedom, while others get set free by their owners, but not many.

"Anyway, I did not have any money and Miss Eliza wanted more of it, so no more time to wait around, I had to leave right then. I had to go alone.

"I was pretty scared that first night 'cause I was told there was a white woman who would help me. Now, at that time most white people I knew either owned me or whipped me or both. But I had to trust someone, so I stopped and knocked on that closed door.

Let me tell you, James, I was scared about as much as you were going into that river.

"But when she saw me at the door she opened it wide, took me in, gave me some water with bread and cheese, and then told me to go out in the yard and sweep up some dirt. She told me the best place to hide sometimes is in plain sight where everyone can see you. No one would think you were a runaway slave if you were sweeping the yard.

"When her husband got back at dark from working his fields, he put me in his wagon, threw a cover over me, and took me 10 miles up the road to the next house. I do not remember exactly how many places I stayed at that trip, or people who helped me, but a good number of both.

"Finally, guess it was about 10 days or so later, I got to Mr. Thomas Garrett's house," she said. "Tomorrow Spenser will take us to visit him again, which I have done many times.

Thomas Garrett

That time, since I had no shoes, my feet were near frozen solid. In a way that's good 'cause when I stepped on a thorn or spiny gum ball I did not feel it so much.

Mr. Thomas put my feet in warm water to thaw out," Harriet went on. "Then he wrapped them up in warm towels while he gave me some hot soup. Next day he gave me a fresh pair of shoes for walking.

"But from Wilmington where he lived he carried me in his wagon across the river and up the road into Pennsylvania, to a place where I was not a slave; a place where I was free.

"When I found I had crossed that line, I looked at my hands to see if I was the same person. There was such a glory over everything; the sun came like gold through the trees, and over the fields, and I felt like I was in heaven."

"Then, when I finally got to Philadelphia, which was the center of the Promised Land then, and met Mr. William Still,

William Still

who took down in a book the names of almost all the slaves who escaped to Philadelphia from the south, I got to thinking about my family.

"I was a stranger in a strange land," said Harriet, "my father, my mother, my brothers and sisters, and friends were down in Maryland. But I was free, and they should be free."

Harriet was again interrupted, but this time by Sarah, little Jane's mother. "Miss Harriet, how in the world you live with no money or friends to help you?"

"I found jobs as a maid or cook for big hotels or for people who had plenty of money to pay me," she replied. "Then later during summers I worked cleaning rooms in hotels down in Cape May. It was a place on the ocean where rich people rested and took vacations. I saved most all the money."

"Not too long after I escaped I heard from people in Baltimore that Kessiah, my niece, and her two young children, were going to be auctioned in Cambridge near where I grew up. Her husband John Bowley, who was a free man, and me talked through friends and decided what to do."

"By the way, James," pausing and looking over at the young boy listening closely to every word Harriet said, "Kessiah's son is named James, like you, and about your age."

James' mother Bess said, "Well ain't that something, maybe someday you boys meet up in the Promised Land." James looked pleased, and Harriet continued.

"Me and John worked up this plan. He went to the sale as a free black man— which he was— and bid high on his wife and children. Then, when the auction broke for lunch he quietly took them away before the slave sellers collected their money. John took his family to a nearby house of a friend. When the auctioneers could not find them the family left Cambridge later that night on a small boat operated by John, an experienced sailor.

"They went up the Chesapeake Bay to Baltimore, a dangerous journey, with some help from John's friends along the way. I met them in Baltimore and took them to Philadelphia where they were safer."

"Where are they now?" asked James. "Maybe we could go there too. It would be nice to have a friend, 'specially one with my name."

"That would be nice, James," said Harriet. "But a lot has changed since they got to the north."

I could see Harriet needed a break, and perhaps a sip of water or some coffee. She had probably talked longer than she had in quite a while, but I wanted to hear more before she rested for the night.

"Let me explain what Miss Harriet's talking about," I said, indicating the coffee pot to Harriet. "The year after she escaped on the freedom train north, the government changed the law to stop slaves from running away to the north.

"They passed a law called the Fugitive Slave Act, which let slave hunters come north and catch any runaway slaves and take them back to the south. This meant that no escaped slave—like Harriet or all of you—could be safe anywhere in the country, and even free Negro people could be hunted and taken to the south and made slaves.

"This meant the Promised Land," I said, "had to be moved further north—into Canada. Canada, which is much farther away from Maryland and other slave states, outlawed slavery many years ago. So the Underground Railroad could not end in Pennsylvania or New York, but had to run farther, which meant slaves had to travel more distance to be free."

I continued, "This has made it much harder, and it takes new runaways longer to reach safety. Even slaves who had escaped earlier and already lived in the north were not safe, and many of them moved on up to Canada too."

"What's it like in Canada Mr. Spenser?" asked Jane, who was much too young to understand the discussion, but who understood she would be living in a place called Canada.

"Well Jane," Harriet picked up, "it sometimes gets cold, but children play in the snow and throw it at each other. And there are lots of children to play with, and no one will ever again whip your momma, or hurt you. But because it's pretty far away, it will take us more time to get there."

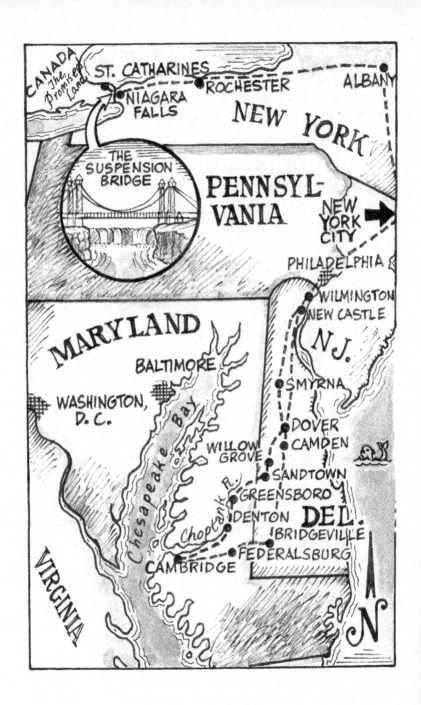

I still had a couple of questions for Harriet. I had heard during meetings of local abolitionists that there were many free black people, as well as some slaves, who thought the best way to really be free was for Negroes to 'colonize' part of Africa, which is where they came from. It was thought they could live free and in peace if they got away from white people.

"Harriet," I said, "with so many Negroes leaving this country for freedom in Canada, the Promised Land, what do you think about slaves returning to Africa? Does that make any sense to you? Quite a few already have left."

---

* Editor's note: The new nation of Liberia on the west coast of Africa was first established in 1847 by and for free blacks, and 'colonization' of Africa was heatedly discussed for years after this, until the Union recognized Liberia's independence in 1862. Initially 15,000 people settled in Liberia, now there are more than four and a half million.

"No, no sense at all," she said. "Let me explain with a story. A man sowed onions and garlic on his land to feed his cattle and increase his dairy production; but he soon learned that the butter was too strong and would not sell. And so he decided to sow clover instead. But then he found the wind had blown the onion and garlic seeds all over his field. Just so, the white people had got the Negro here to do their drudgery, and now they are trying to root us out and send us to Africa. They can't do it; we're rooted here, and they can't pull us up."

"Mr. Spenser," said Sam, "it like Miss Harriet say...this is who we are and where we always be. It is our country too."

While I found this most interesting, and could have discussed it much longer, I was even more interested in how many of Harriet's family she had been able to help escape from slavery.

"Since you started on the Underground Railroad," I asked, "have you been able to help your whole family escape from slavery?"

"Some," she replied, "but not all. As I mentioned, my sisters Linah and Soph were sold south when I was just a teenager. I had another older sister—Mariah Ritty— who was sold when I was just a baby. I did help my brothers Ben, Robert and Henry— with some of their families—get out.

"It was Christmas of 1854 and Miss Eliza was said to be selling them soon. I was able to get word to them I was coming, and then I had to hurry to get there before they were sold. Mostly I took trains and boats, no time to do much walking. I got there on Christmas eve, and first thing I saw was a notice all three brothers were to be sold the day after Christmas."

I could see she was remembering back before she continued. "I got word to my brothers that we would meet and then go up to where our parents lived in Poplar Neck. We would leave from there.

"When my brother Robert did not arrive on time, we had to leave for Poplar Neck without him. His wife Mary was due to have a baby very soon, and it was hard on Robert to leave her and his other two young children.

---

* **Editor's note:** Mary gave birth to a baby girl that night, who she named Harriet. Robert, after finally explaining to his wife that he was leaving, had to walk out and leave his family, not knowing if he would ever see them again. Separation and destruction of families was probably the worst, most devastating part of slavery—even worse than the beatings and whippings.

But for us time was scarce so we could not delay. Fortunately, we were staying a night near our parent's home, and Robert had time to catch up with us.

"We got to a place behind my parents cabin and stayed there in the fodder house where we could see through spaces in the wall our mother smoking her pipe and rocking in her chair. Every so often she would look down the road for her children who she believed were coming to have a family Christmas dinner."

"Why didn't you go inside for dinner and to say goodbye to your mother?" asked James.

"Well," said Harriet, "I don't know about your Momma over there, but 'Old Rit'—that's what everyone called her—she was not one to keep quiet. If she saw us and knew we were leaving she would make a big commotion, likely wake up the master. She wanted her family with her, not up north.

"Now my Daddy Ben," Harriet said, "he knew what we were doing and brought us some food that night before we left.

Not much of a Christmas dinner, but we were happy to get it. My father was one of the most honest, respected black men on the Eastern Shore, everyone knew he always told the truth.

"So when he brought us the food he covered his eyes with a bandana and did not look at us. Then he could truthfully say he did not see us before we left. Otherwise if he lied he was afraid they would see it on his face."

"Miss Harriet," James asked, "did Robert take his children with you to the Promised Land?"

"He did not, I'm afraid, his wife was too weak to travel" said Harriet. "But my brother Ben's fiancée Jane went with us. Fact is Jane Kane was owned by Mr. Horatio Jones like you," looking at Bess and Sam, who immediately nodded that they knew Jane.

"Why, I know Jane, she worked with me in the fields," said Bess. "I never did know if she made it north. Knew she was seeing your brother, should have figured it out. Glad she did."

Harriet went on, "We talked some that trip. Jane said same as you about Mr. Horatio. She said he was 'the worst man in the country'. Said that he beat her brother until his back was as raw as a piece of beef. Said he beat Jane until the blood ran from her mouth and nose, and then locked her in a closet until she almost suffocated. Jane said he took away their clothes so they could not run away."

"How your Momma find out her children gone?" asked James.

"Daddy walked down the road with us when we left," said Harriet. "He took the arms of his sons Ben and Robert with his blindfold on while we all walked. Then, when we all hugged him and said goodbye we left Ben standing in the road. He later told me he listened to our footfalls until he could not hear them. Then he walked home to tell Old Rit. Sure glad I was not there when he did.

"Not much more to tell about that trip," said Harriet. "We did not have anything bad happen, and got to St. Catharine's in Canada a bit later that year." Then, looking at James and Jane, Harriet told them that with God's guidance they would be in St. Catharine's soon, and there they would make new friends, and go to school and learn to read and write.

"But what about Old Rit and Mr. Ben, your Momma and Daddy?" asked James. "Did you go back for them? Are they in Canada?"

'Maybe Miss Harriet not want to talk about them; maybe that not a question she want," said Sam, afraid they could be dead or still in Maryland and slaves. Sam knew James sometimes asked too many questions.

"It's okay Sam," said Harriet, "they are doing just fine now. With most of their children up in Canada I persuaded them to go with me to the Promised Land. They said they would go, maybe because people started thinking my father was an agent for the Underground Railroad, and who knew what they would do to him. But more, I think, because they sure missed their family, which they knew was not coming back to Maryland.

"Because they were both old and in their 70s, they could not do much walking,

so I had to take them mostly by wagon and train, and we could not move fast, so it took a while to get them to Canada.

"That first winter in Canada was real cold and icy, and they were often sick and unhappy," Harriet said. "So I took them back to where I lived in Auburn, New York, and they did better there."

Harriet paused, asked for some water, and then continued: "My youngest brother Moses came north a little after me, but don't know anymore where he is. He went his own way.

"And my sister Rachel is dead," she said, "I went back to get her and her two young ones when I heard Rachel was gone with God. We planned for her children to meet me and we would leave that night. But it was terrible snow and hard wind, and they never did come. I had to leave without them.

"I never saw them again," she said. "Maybe they were sold south, can't say. That's all I know, and probably ever going to know. When you're running a train, you can't wait until all the passengers get on board. You have to leave on time."

"And," I said, "we have to leave on time tomorrow morning for Wilmington to meet Mr. Garrett. We will leave a little before dawn in my wagon. You will all be hidden underneath a hard plywood cover."

When they were all in the wagon I would lay on top of the plywood a half-cord of cut wood. The baby would be given some laudanum to sleep, and I would drive the wagon with Charley doing the heavy work. The trip would be uncomfortable for Harriet and her passengers, but they'd all been through much worse.

Harriet agreed with the timing and the plan, and at that point I thanked her for telling me her stories about the work she did on the Underground Railroad.

The secret railroad continued for several more years, but neither Harriet Tubman nor I spent much more time with it. Before she could make another trip we were at war.

№ 4

John Brown's Plan

After I dropped Harriet and her passengers off at Mr. Thomas Garrett's house in Wilmington, Delaware, which later led to safety for James and Jane and their families in Canada, none of us could know how much everything was about to change. Soon the north and the south would be fighting a bloody Civil War between the states.

Although at this point the war was more than a year away, I only saw Harriet occasionally when I would run across her at meetings of abolitionists and we would catch up with one another. The debate over slavery and how to end it was becoming more and more heated.

One group of abolitionists believed that slavery could be overcome by peaceful, ongoing resistance. A second group of activists strongly disagreed with this and said the only way to end slavery was to conduct an armed uprising which would spread across the south and eventually provide slaves the freedom and justice they deserved.

One man who was a leader of the faction that believed in a violent overthrow of slavery was John Brown. Brown thought that slavery had gone on much too long, and that all his fellow abolitionists did was talk, talk, talk. He wanted action, and he had a plan.

John Brown

But before he could go to war against slave owners and pro-slavery sympathizers he had to raise enough money to undertake such an effort—which included arming his troops. He also had to recruit the troops to do it.

For several years he traveled across the north asking for support and money. Even those who were skeptical of the success of such an armed effort applauded his goal to end slavery. I was at several meetings where Mr. Brown spoke and asked for financial support of his plan, which at its end would have established a free slave state in the western areas of Virginia and Maryland.

Of course I did not have the resources to support him if I had wanted to, which I did not. I believed that the only path to success was not in violence but in persistence.

When I visited with Harriet at a meeting of abolitionists near Boston, we talked some about John Brown, who I knew held Harriet in the highest regard.

I asked Harriet whether she supported Brown and his plans for violently attacking slave owners, and she surprised me with her reply. "I have met with him several times here and in Canada, and I believe he is fully committed to eliminating slavery. He is a man of God, and he is willing to fight and even die for the freedom of slaves. I have come to respect him a great deal."

"Are you going to join him in armed battle?" I asked, somewhat surprised at her clear respect for this man.

"He wants me to, Spenser," she replied. "I have helped him with recruiting in Canada where, as you know, many escaped fugitives have settled. I introduced him to some, and many were persuaded to volunteer if his plan happens.

"I have also discussed with him the Underground Railroad network of free blacks and slaves, and others like you Spenser, who believe in abolishing slavery. He thinks this will help him recruit men for his raid."

"I guess," I said, "you have to decide where you can do the most good. It's a decision we all have to make. Just most of us cannot do as much good as you can. You've already done so much."

Harriet looked a little troubled, and for a moment she was quiet and thoughtful. "I worry a lot about my parents Ben and Old Rit. I do not have much money to support them, and they need whatever help I can give. Mr. Seward sold me some land and a house in Auburn on good terms and I moved my parents and some others in to live with me. They did not do too well up there in Canada with the cold weather blowing off Lake Ontario, with them so old.

---

* Editor's note: Harriet Tubman was always poor, and often lived in poverty. She raised some money to support her activities, but it was never enough to support herself and her family. Nearly everything she had she gave to others. At one point they had to burn the wood in the fences on her property for firewood to heat their home. On another occasion they had no food to eat, so Harriet took an empty basket to the market. When a kindly butcher saw nothing in the bag he gave her a soup bone. Then others gave her meat, potatoes and vegetables. Harriet's family and boarders did not go hungry that night. While the community often supported her, she never begged for help.

William H. Seward was a United States Senator, abolitionist and frequent financial sponsor and friend with his wife Frances to Harriet Tubman. The Sewards lived near Tubman in Auburn in northern New York. Auburn was near one of the primary routes of the Underground Railroad. Later, after Abraham Lincoln was elected President, Seward became his Secretary of State and a trusted advisor.

William Seward

I heard later in abolitionist circles that John Brown thought Harriet was one of the most impressive leaders he had ever met.

He called her "General Tubman" for her leadership ability, and he considered her important to his success.

But Harriet in the end did not join with John Brown on his plan to violently overthrow slavery. Although she never said, to me or anyone else, why she did not join him, I think it was largely because of her love for and sense of responsibility for her family. She knew that without her many in her family, especially her parents, would be lost.

John Brown, on the other hand, was moving forward with his plan to attack the federal armory *[where a large arsenal of guns was kept]* at Harper's Ferry. He hoped to capture enough weapons from it to arm a slave rebellion. He expected slaves to join him as he swept through the south.

While, I am told, the plan called for more than 4,000 slaves and free black men to join the effort, Brown only had 21 including his three sons for his attack on the armory. *[At this time the total number of slaves in the country was about four million; nearly all of them lived in the south]*. His attack was defeated by a company of U.S. marines, with Colonel Robert E. Lee in charge. *[Lee later became the Commanding General of the Confederate armies during the Civil War].*

Robert E. Lee

I was very pleased that Harriet had not taken part in the raid, for she likely would have been killed or captured and executed if she had. The raid did not succeed, and John Brown and several of his men were hanged for treason at the end of 1859.

---

* **Editor's note:** To this day, historians disagree on whether John Brown was a hero and martyr who gave his life to free slaves, or a madman—even a terrorist. About 20 years after Brown's execution, Frederick Douglass wrote, "His zeal in the cause of my race was far greater than mine—it was as the burning sun to my taper *[candle]* light—mine was bounded by time, his stretched away to the boundless shores of eternity. I could live for a slave, but he could die for him." Harriet Tubman said after Brown's death that "he did more in dying, than 100 men would in living."

Harriet
(and Spenser)
Go to War

President Lincoln's election was an issue on which Harriet and I differed somewhat. It seemed to me that she thought that Abraham Lincoln was moving too slowly to free the slaves, and that maybe he was not fully committed to freedom for all Negroes.

Abraham Lincoln

I, on the other hand, had not a doubt that the new president would end slavery as soon as he could. Harriet, despite her concerns and impatience for freedom, was totally dedicated to the Union and the war that was soon to start between the north and the south.

---

* Editor's note: When Lincoln was elected in 1860 northern states and southern states were deeply divided on the issue of slavery.

Lincoln's election proved to be the final straw for the states in the south that grew cotton and totally relied on slave labor to pick and harvest it. Between the time Lincoln was elected and was inaugurated as president seven states in the deep south had seceded *[become independent Confederate states and, they said, no longer part of the Union—the United States]*.

Four more states seceded after Lincoln took office on March 4, 1861. Although Lincoln repeatedly said during his campaign for president, and restated in his inaugural address, that he had no intention of outlawing slavery where it already existed, pro-slavery supporters wanted to expand slavery into many of the new states being established in the territories in the Midwest and West.

The war actually began a little more than a month after President Lincoln took office. On April 12, Confederate troops began shelling Fort Sumter, which was on a small island in the harbor in Charleston, South Carolina. A day later, before any additional Union soldiers could be sent to help those at the fort, Fort Sumter was overtaken by southern troops.

The attack on Fort Sumter caused immediate outrage in the north.

Within weeks President Lincoln was calling for thousands of volunteers to join the Union army.

---

* **Editor's note:** The Civil War did in fact end slavery, but not until it became the most deadly American war of all time, with estimates on the number killed falling between 620 thousand and 750 thousand total killed on both sides. When it finally ended the war had lasted four years.

I told Maggie and my children that it was my duty to fight for the freedom of all slaves. While my family was worried for my safety, they all understood and supported my decision. I soon left to volunteer to fight for my country.

At this time neither black men nor cats were permitted to serve proudly as soldiers or to fight in battle. By the time this changed after the signing of President Lincoln's Emancipation Proclamation more than a year later, both Harriet and I were very busy working to save the lives of sick and wounded Union soldiers. And while Harriet later was assigned to lead soldiers in battle behind enemy lines, most of my own service was as a medical aide.

While I was volunteering to serve for the Union, Harriet was using her long friendship with several abolitionists— especially William Lloyd Garrison in Boston— to volunteer as well. She had been able to secure enough money for her parents and other family to make it through a cold New York winter and believed she could send more money home from her work for the army. So with her family provided for she asked Garrison to help her find a job aiding the Union cause and supporting freedom for her people.

William Lloyd Garrison

It did not take her long to have a meeting with Governor John Andrew of Massachusetts, who used his contacts and influence to have Harriet assigned to the Department of the South near Beaufort, South Carolina. Her long experience communicating with local slaves and their supporters persuaded the governor that she could prove helpful in gathering information that would aid the Union cause.

Very few slaves who escaped to the north like Harriet were permitted to travel south during the war, but her long experience meeting and talking with local slaves and their abolitionist supporters on the Underground Railroad persuaded the governor that she would be valuable in gathering information that would aid the Union cause.

---

* Editor's note: The Department of the South was a unique area in the Confederate south, hundreds of miles from the border between the north and the south. It was controlled by the Union but completely surrounded by the Confederacy.

It was established after the Union navy captured two forts on the South Carolina coast. These defeats for the south persuaded many local plantation owners and other white landowners, along with most remaining southern troops, to leave the area before they were captured or killed. They left behind their estates and many of their slaves, who remained on the land.

Much of this area in South Carolina was in the Port Royal district that included Hilton Head, St. Helena's Island, Sea Island and Beaufort. The Department of the South also included some areas of Georgia and Florida.

Part of her work was to spy on southern people and troops, and report to Union officers any troop movements or preparations for battle she saw or heard about. Because she was raised near a swampy area filled with snakes and insects that carried disease— an area similar to the land around Beaufort— she also would be a nurse.

As coincidence would have it, I was also serving at this same location as a medical assistant for the Union at the local base hospital.

I had worked through abolitionist channels like Harriet did, and finally was provided passage on a Union supply boat headed to Beaufort where I would help care for sick soldiers there. Because there wasn't much fighting taking place in the area at this time, most of the soldiers were hospitalized for disease, not battle wounds.

Nonetheless, soldiers were dying as a result of contaminated water and food, bad sanitation and hygiene and diseases like malaria, smallpox, typhoid and dysentery. Many deadly illnesses were carried by ticks, fleas and mosquitoes. Several of the men I treated told me they would rather die from a bullet than a slow, painful disease that made them delirious [crazy].

Not long after I arrived at the hospital I saw Harriet washing with cool water the feverish bodies of the sick. As she often did when she worked, she sang to the men as she moved from one to another. She had a lovely, strong voice, and I could tell the men found much peace from Harriet's singing of hymns and spirituals which she had sung since she was a child.

Many, many times that year and in the years that followed we would talk about the war, freedom, our families and President Lincoln. I remember one time Harriet talked about what the president needed to do before the north could win the war.

"I would tell that Master Lincoln," she said, "that he needs to set the Negroes free. Suppose that there was a big snake down on the floor. He bite you. Folks all scared that maybe you die. You send for a doctor to cut the poison out of the bite. But that snake, he rolled up there, and while the doctor helping you he bite you again.

"The doctor dig out that bite too, but while the doctor doing it, the snake, he spring up and bite you again; so he keep doing it, till you kill him. That's what Master Lincoln ought to know."

---

* Editor's note: Harriet meant that if President Lincoln did not end slavery, which she compared with a snake, all the problems that came from slavery would remain, and nothing would change.

Another time Harriet told me about a slave who escaped but did not make it to the Promised Land with her family. "Her name," said Harriet, "was Margaret Garner. She and her family tried to escape from a plantation in Kentucky out west. They got to Cincinnati in Ohio when the master and his slave hunters caught them. Before those men could take Mary, Margaret's little girl, away from her she just leaned over and killed her daughter. Ain't nobody, she said, going to make Mary grow up a slave."

---

* **Editor's note:** The story of Margaret Garner became the basis of *Beloved*, a book by Nobel Prize winner Toni Morrison (1987). *Beloved* was later made into a motion picture starring Oprah Winfrey.

I found it hard to believe a mother would kill her own child like that. "Why did she do that?" I asked. "How could she kill her child if she loved her?"

"She did it because she loved her so much," Harriet said. "She would not let that child suffer like she had. If that child could not be free, then she would not live as a slave."

Well, it was not a long time later that President Lincoln issued an executive order—

the Emancipation Proclamation—that led to freedom for most slaves. From that time onward, slaves who lived in the south were free. They were no longer anyone's property. They were free!!!

Of course, their white owners and the slave hunters they hired, and the overseers who whipped them bloody for any reason at all did not agree. To them, nothing had changed, and if they won the war it never would.

But at this time Harriet had much more to do every day than dream about freedom. She was not being paid for the nursing work she did with the soldiers, so in order to support herself and also send some money to care for her parents and family at their home in New York, she had to work almost all day and night long.

She spent most of her time when she was not nursing sick men, cooking, sewing and washing clothes for soldiers. In Beaufort she ran a small eating house where she provided meals to anyone who could afford to pay for a hot, home-cooked meal.

Harriet Tubman also made pies and cakes for sale—wonderful pies and cakes I can swear to—along with ginger bread and root beer.

She paid Negro workers *[called 'contrabands' sometimes by the men and officers because at the time they were no longer slaves but not free either]* to sell her popular sweets to the soldiers, and probably to others who liked sweets and lived nearby. While she was working to make money for herself and family she was also scouting for the most senior officers of the Department.

At first she worked with local slaves and freemen inside of the Department to hear all the local rumors about Confederate troop movements. She developed a network of sources, and recruited additional scouts to gather information.

Later, as she got to know more about the local population and the land—which was like the wetlands where she grew up—she moved behind enemy lines to give the Union officers more valuable information.

After about three months, early in 1863, Harriet and I left the hospital one afternoon for a short walk to get some clean air. She seemed excited.

"I have just met," she said, "an officer who served with John Brown in Kansas when he was fighting against slavery there. His name is Colonel James Montgomery. He has been assigned here to take over and build the Second South Carolina volunteers.

---

* Editor's note: This was a newly created unit of African American troops made up of free blacks and slaves recently freed by the Emancipation Proclamation.

I remembered that John Brown had asked Harriet to join him for his disastrous raid at Harper's Ferry in Virginia *[now West Virginia]*, after which he was hanged for treason. "Did you know Colonel Montgomery before you saw him here?"

"No," she said. "But John Brown mentioned him to me and said he was a 'fighting man', in his words. I hope I am able to work with him and his troops in the future."

And it was only a few months later that Harriet did indeed work with Col. James Montgomery in one of the most important and successful raids of the war up to that point.

As Harriet later recounted to me, Colonel Montgomery asked her to visit him in his headquarters tent sometime in May 1863 not long after he arrived in the camp. He and the Second South Carolina along with the First South Carolina regiment led by Col. Thomas Higginson, had recently returned from an attack on Jacksonville, Florida.

"Harriet," said Col. Montgomery, "it is good to meet you. I've heard so much about you from John Brown, Col. Higginson and General Hunter."

"Colonel," Harriet said, "I've heard of your fighting and support for freedom from John Brown many times. I thank you for the work you have done, and I hope I can help you now that you are here."

"You may know that we have just returned from an attack on Jacksonville that unfortunately did not provide us the results we wanted," Montgomery said. "While our soldiers *[among the first African American soldiers, as a result of the Emancipation Proclamation, to fight in the Civil War]* fought bravely and with honor, we did not accomplish our primary objective."

"What was that Colonel?" asked Harriet.

Colonel Montgomery replied, "We have been authorized to recruit another regiment of Negro troops to join with Col. Higginson's First South Carolina. I am the commander of this second regiment, the Second South Carolina.

"While General Hunter was recruiting the first regiment, he found that he needed to free more slaves in order to recruit more soldiers.

"The attack on Jacksonville," Montgomery continued, "was intended to free many more slaves who could fight for the Union and for their freedom.

"However, before we reached Jacksonville, most of the slave owners had taken their able-bodied slaves and left the area. While we were able to free about 30 men who could fight, we need many more."

Harriet knew the colonel had something more he wanted to ask her, so she quietly waited for him to continue.

"I would like your help," said Colonel Montgomery, "you know more about this territory than anyone else in the camp. You are strong and tough and a leader. John Brown always referred to you as 'General Tubman', and he said you were the best leader he ever knew.

"I want you to plan and lead a raid with me up the Combahee River," the colonel said, "to free as many slaves as we can find, and to destroy as much of the south's supplies of food, textiles and crops, and their ability to wage war against freedom, as we can.

"I want you to join with me to lead the men of the Second South Carolina on a mission behind enemy lines to accomplish our most important objective—to free slaves and to take them right off their plantations where they still live in chains." Here Colonel Montgomery stopped, and watched Harriet carefully.

"Colonel," she said at once, "I accept your offer, and I will fight beside you and your men, and give up my life if it is God's will. This raid will succeed. My scouts know every turn of that river, and they can talk with slaves up and down the river so the enemy cannot surprise us."

∗ Editor's note: Because of Harriet's deep knowledge of the enemy-held territory beyond the land close to Beaufort, and her natural leadership abilities, Col. Montgomery and Harriet Tubman undertook the first and likely only Union attack on rebel forces in the South jointly led by an African American woman.

At this point, Harriet told me later, Colonel Montgomery told her how many boats and men she would have, and when the General wanted them to leave for their trip up the Combahee to free slaves, and to recruit soldiers.

They would leave at night, and there would be three steam-driven gun boats—the John Adams, the Harriet A. Weed and the Sentinel. Three hundred men would travel with them on the boats, and it was Harriet's first job to make certain the boats were not sunk or destroyed by mines *[called torpedoes at the time]* planted in the river by the southern forces.

It was also important that rebel snipers along the river did not halt or delay their journey, and took as few lives as possible. Harriet sent several of her scouts along the banks of the Combahee River to locate any southern troops or snipers. They made good use of local sources, who they recruited to help.

The lead boat was the John Adams, where Colonel Montgomery and Harriet Tubman stood on the deck to lead the surprise attack. Walter D. Plowden was Harriet's chief scout, and he carefully led the boats around and through the mines spread across the river.

Only one mistake by Plowden—missing just one mine—and the entire effort might have ended in failure and death for many, including both Colonel Montgomery and Harriet.

But Plowden did not run his boat across a mine, or make any other mistake, and the boats and soldiers made it far up the river to the site of several plantations. The Union forces knew where the plantations and their warehouses, barns, fields and stockpiles were located because Harriet's scouts had been there and reported the locations to the officers.

Facing little armed resistance, the Union troops captured as many farm animals and stocks of rice, corn and other crops as they could carry. What they could not take on their ships they burned, including houses, barns and storage sheds. They flooded the fields that soon would have produced food for the southern troops.

Then Colonel Montgomery destroyed the local bridge and ordered the boats' whistles blown to alert the slaves to come down to the river and leave on the boats for freedom. They came by the hundreds.

Harriet told me she saw men carrying young children, chairs, chickens and whatever personal items they could grab. She said she saw one mother with a baby in her arms, another small child hanging onto her waist and two others holding their mother's dress as she ran. Another woman had grabbed a hot pot of rice still steaming from being cooked. She was carrying it on a wrap on top of her head.

At first some were afraid to board the ships, and others were scrambling to get on board. Harriet decided the best thing she could do to encourage them and reduce their fear was to sing to them. Spirituals and gospel music was a common language, and after Harriet with her loud and beautiful voice began singing, everything settled down and it became much smoother.

The steam boats, now packed tight with more than 700 slaves, crops, livestock and personal items slowly steamed back toward the camp. Once again Plowden kept the boats from hitting the mines, and nearly all the Union men returned safely.

The mission had been successful beyond all expectations, and dozens— probably hundreds—of new recruits signed up to fight for the Union.

Not long after the successful raid up the Combahee River, another attack was scheduled, this time on Charleston. After days of bombings and fighting, the Union forces suffered a significant defeat. While Harriet supported the effort, it was not as a soldier but as a nurse to help the wounded and dying.

At this battle it was the 54th Massachusetts that took most of the massive counter attack by the Confederate troops defending the city and its harbor. The Union's dead, wounded and missing in action numbered more than 1,500 while the Confederates lost fewer than 200 men. Harriet later said in a remarkable, almost poetic description, what she saw in that battle.

"And then we saw the lightning," she said, "and that was the guns; and then we heard the thunder, and that was the big guns; and then we heard the rain falling, and that was the drops of blood falling;

and when we came to get in the crops,
it was the dead that we reaped."

The fighting in and around Charleston
continued into September, with Harriet
working nearly around the clock caring
for the soldiers. Although she never said,
or complained, she must have been
totally exhausted.

Harriet's work in the Department of
the South continued almost until the end
of the war, but she went on to other locations
to support the black soldiers who had been
injured, as did I. We had few opportunities
to visit in the remaining months of the war.

The war eventually ended for all of us.
On April 9, 1865, General Robert E. Lee
surrendered to General Ulysses S. Grant
at Appomattox Courthouse in Virginia.
Only six days later, President Lincoln
was assassinated *[killed]* while watching
a play at Ford's Theater with his wife
near the U.S. Capitol.

President Lincoln had led our Union
through a long and difficult war to protect
and preserve the Union, and he had been
the leader who had set free the slaves.

It was terribly sad that he did not live to see the fruits of his hard labor and love for his country.

After the war I returned to New Castle, Delaware, to my family. And, with no need for me to continue as a stationmaster on the Underground Railroad, I was able to continue my work making fine furniture.

Soon after the war ended I crafted a strong—and handsome if I do say— rocking chair for Harriet's mother 'Old Rit'. Harriet let me know later it was her mother's favorite chair.

№ 6 The Rest of Harriet's Story

Editor's Postscript

This is the end of Spenser's story, but it is not the end of Harriet Tubman's story. She had much more to do, much more to contribute to her people and her country.

As the war ended, Harriet was persuaded by several nurses to go to Fortress Monroe in Hampton, Virginia, where there was a large hospital that cared for wounded African American soldiers. When she arrived she was shocked by the abuses and neglect of these black veterans of the war, who fought for the freedom they had every right to.

But, mostly because of poor care and less care, these black men were dying at two and a half times the rate of white soldiers, which Harriet decided to expose and she hoped to improve.

She traveled to Washington where she visited Secretary of State Seward, who had sold her on generous terms her farm in Auburn, New York. Although he had been seriously injured the same night President Lincoln had been killed, he met Harriet and sent her to the Surgeon General *[government's medical director]* Dr. Joseph Barnes.

Although Barnes tried to help, little was actually done and Harriet decided she could make better use of her time with her family in Auburn, so she returned to New York.

As she was traveling home on a train between Philadelphia and New York City, she was seated on a train car reserved just for white people. When the conductor told her to leave and go to another car where black travelers were permitted to sit, she refused and grabbed hold of her seat.

Although Harriet was stronger than the conductor, and he could not remove her, he got other men to help him. Together they tore her out of her seat, breaking her arm because she would not yield.

Then they threw her roughly onto another car, breaking or cracking several of her ribs. When the men called her 'colored', or worse, she made it clear to them she was to be addressed as a 'Negro' or 'black' woman. She was proud of her race, and did not easily tolerate it being demeaned or diminished.

While slavery had ended *[legally with passage of the 13th Amendment to the Constitution passed in 1865]*, bigotry, segregation and violence had not. At this time, and for a year after, many states passed laws called 'Black Codes.' While these laws varied some between states, in general they were designed to help whites maintain control over blacks, much as they had during slavery. One writer later called it"slavery by another name."

Under these laws African Americans were not permitted to own property, or their own business or guns and other arms.

If they were found to be 'vagrant'—which meant anytime a white man wanted to say a black man should not be where he was—they could be arrested and forced to do involuntary labor.

Despite her beating, which prevented her from physical labor for several months, when Harriet got home to Auburn little had changed. Her parents were aging, and there was little money to support them or their home.

For the rest of her life, as always had been true, Harriet lived in near-poverty. Her well-deserved pension for her service during the Civil War would not be provided to her until late in her life. She and her family were largely supported by contributions from wealthy families who had long known Harriet and respected her work.

In addition, boarders sometimes paid a little rent for living at her farm, and for several years she and her husband had income from making bricks for houses. Occasionally she would earn fees for speaking at meetings on behalf of women's suffrage *[giving women the vote]*.

One of the boarders she rented a room to was Nelson Davis. Davis had been a slave in North Carolina and after he escaped he settled in New York. During the war he had enlisted in a USCT regiment *[United States Colored Troops]*, and had fought bravely in battle in Florida.

Harriet's first husband—John Tubman— who she had married before she escaped on the Underground Railroad, had been shot and killed in a fight. So, after more than 20 years she was free to remarry, which she did with Nelson Davis.

Davis was more than 20 years younger than Harriet, but he was suffering from tuberculosis, a disease that could not be cured and which eventually killed him. However, it is likely that Harriet considered it a blessing to have a husband to share life with every day until his death.

A little before the new century began in 1900, and as Harriet approached the age of 80, she received an honor and an invitation that always made her proud. Harriet Tubman's reputation had stretched across the Atlantic Ocean to Great Britain and beyond. For the celebration of Queen Victoria's Diamond Jubilee *[50th anniversary]* in 1897 Queen Victoria invited Harriet to come to the celebration as her guest.

Harriet declined based on her frailties, finances and age, but she was no doubt pleased to receive from the Queen a commemorative silver medal and the gift of a beautiful white shawl, which she used for the rest of her life. *[It is now displayed at the National Museum of African American History and Culture in Washington, DC].*

A year later the ongoing headaches and seizures that plagued Harriet since she was a child and was hit in the head by the weight thrown by the overseer in the local store became unbearable. She could not sleep, and could hardly think without terrible pain.

While traveling in Boston she visited a hospital, talked with a brain surgeon and asked him to operate on her head to relieve the pain. He said he would, but when he offered her pain killers for the surgery she declined. I just "lay down," she said, "like a lamb before the slaughter and he sawed open my skull. It feels more comfortable now."

When asked if she suffered much, she said, "Yes, sir, it hurt of course." But she had preferred biting on a bullet like the soldiers who had suffered amputations during the war, and who she had held down during surgery. The surgeon's grandson later said his grandfather told him "she lay motionless as a log, mumbling prayers through teeth clenched on a bullet."

"I got up and put on my bonnet and started to walk home," she said, "but my legs kind of give out under me, and they sent for an ambulance and sent me home."

Harriet did indeed get home, and in time recovered from the surgery on her head.

She had planned to build an infirmary and home for aged Negroes, but as characterized all of her life, she was unable to provide the funds required. Fortunately, the Auburn AME Zion Church took an interest and worked with Harriet to build the 'Harriet Tubman Home for Aged and Infirm Negroes'. It was opened in 1908.

She continued for several more years to attend suffrage meetings in New York and Boston, and spoke on the subject when she was able to attend meetings.

As Harriet became older and more infirm, eventually unable to walk, she became a resident of the home she had dreamed of and worked so hard to establish.
She died on March 10, 1913.

An Appreciation

Harriet Tubman was a force far beyond anything we can imagine today. She did not write her legacy in a book, or on Facebook. I'm sure she did not have either the time or the interest to consider that she might one day become an icon *[hero]* who would have her picture on her country's $20 bill.

Harriet Tubman did not play politics—although she understood them very well— and she did not make herself look good so that future generations would applaud her and remember her.

Harriet Tubman

What she believed—and what drove her—was that she had the right to be free, the right to live and love and be equal to anyone else, white or black.

If President Abraham Lincoln was the political muscle behind overcoming slavery in our country, Harriet Tubman was the leader in the trenches. Lincoln and Harriet Tubman never met, but it is certain that his effort to free slaves while holding the Union together would not have succeeded without Harriet Tubman and others like her.

There really are not, however, any others like Harriet Tubman. Her contributions to her race and gender, and to the values of freedom, human dignity and social justice that we now hold dear, were unmatched then or now.

---

* **Editor's note:** The Preamble to the Declaration of Independence starts: "We hold these truths to be self-evident, that **all men are created equal,** that they are endowed by their Creator with certain unalienable Rights, that among these are Life, Liberty and the pursuit of Happiness." *—July 4, 1776*

There have been few people in history who have accomplished as much as Harriet Tubman. And all she wanted was that she and her family could live free, that slavery would end and that African American people would be considered and treated as equal to all others in the Promised Land of America.

Now, more than 240 years after the Declaration of Independence was written, and more than 150 years after slavery was abolished, liberty and equality still need more work.

The last bridge to freedom

Frederick Douglass takes Harriet Tubman and passengers from the United States to the promised land in Canada.

Glossary

People, Terms, Events & Places

People

Abraham Lincoln
President of the United States (the Union) during the Civil War. His support for abolishing slavery and his authorship of the Emancipation Proclamation led to freedom for all slaves. He was killed by an assassin on April 15, 1865, six days after the war ended.

Anthony Thompson
A wealthy slave owner in Dorchester County, MD, who owned Harriet Tubman's parents, Ben and Rit Ross.

Araminta Ross
Harriet Tubman's birth name. Called Minty for short, she changed her name to Harriet Tubman when she married John Tubman circa 1844.

Ben Ross
Harriet Tubman's father and a slave who was considered by everyone a totally honest man and also a highly skilled worker as a timberman. Harriet took him to freedom with her mother

Rit during one of her estimated 13 trips to Dorchester County, MD, on the Underground Railroad *[UGRR]*.

Col. James Montgomery
Regimental leader of the Second South Carolina black troops. He asked Harriet Tubman to lead a raid to free slaves from plantations up the Combahee River in South Carolina. This was likely the only Union action led jointly by an African American woman.

Col. Thomas Higginson
Regimental leader of the First South Carolina black troops, whose men participated in a raid against Confederate troops in Jacksonville, Florida.

Dr. Joseph Barnes
The Surgeon General of the Union who met with Harriet Tubman about the poor treatment black soldiers at Fortress Monroe were receiving; their mortality rates *[death rates]* were two and a half times those of white soldiers.

Edward Brodess
The slave owner in Dorchester County, MD, who owned Harriet Tubman. In addition to abusing her physically and emotionally from an early age, he tried to sell her south like he had sold her older sisters before her.

Eliza Brodess
Edward's wife, who after his death was close to selling Harriet to the south before Harriet escaped on the Underground Railroad.

Frederick Douglass
A literate African American who escaped slavery and became a prominent abolitionist. He was a friend of Harriet Tubman's and helped take her passengers to freedom in Canada as a stationmaster in Rochester, NY.

General David Hunter
A commanding general of the Department of the South, where Harriet Tubman led a raid up the Combahee River in South Carolina. He was a committed abolitionist and early-on encouraged the Union to arm black soldiers and permit them to fight.

Harriet Beecher Stowe
An abolitionist and the author of *Uncle Tom's Cabin (1852)* which told her mostly-white readers about the inhumane treatment of slaves. It provoked a loud and widespread outrage, and contributed to the northern commitment to end slavery.

Harriet Greene Ross
Harriet Tubman's mother, often called 'Old Rit.' She and her husband Ben were taken to freedom

by her daughter after many of her children had already reached the Promised Land. Ben and Old Rit lived with their daughter for several years before they died.

Harriet Tubman

A former Maryland slave who escaped to the north, and then returned at great risk to her own life many times, to take her family and others to freedom. Perhaps the most successful conductor on the Underground Railroad—she never lost a passenger.

Horatio Jones

A local slaveowner in Dorchester County known for being especially cruel and abusive to his slaves. Harriet's brother Ben's fiancée—Jane Kane—owned by Horatio Jones, escaped with several of Harriet's brothers.

Jane Kane

Escaped with Harriet and lived with her in Auburn, NY for many years. She often led the household when Harriet was away. After moving to New York she changed her name to Catherine Stewart.

John Brown

An abolitionist who led an armed revolt against slavery at Harper's Ferry, VA [now WVA]. He considered Harriet Tubman one of the strongest leaders he ever met, and called her 'General Tubman'. He asked her to join his insurrection, but while supportive she did not join him for the attack.

John Tubman
Harriet Tubman's first husband, a free black, whose name she took. He declined to join with her to escape and years later was killed in a fight.

Kessiah
A niece of Harriet Tubman, who with Harriet's help and guidance escaped with John Bowley and her two children immediately after she had been sold at a slave auction in Cambridge, MD.

Mariah Ritty, Soph, Linah, Moses, Ben, Robert, Henry and Rachel
Harriet Tubman's brothers and sisters, some of whom escaped to the north while others were sold south.

Margaret Garner
A Kentucky slave who tried to escape to the north through Ohio. When she and her family were captured by her owner and slave hunters, she killed her small daughter Mary to keep her from living in slavery.

Nat Turner

The leader of a slave revolt in 1831 in Virginia.
It resulted in the deaths of about 60 whites.
In retaliation white militias and mobs killed
more than 200 blacks who had little or nothing
to do with the rebellion. Turner and his followers
were caught and executed, although Turner
alone escaped capture for two months.
The revolt fed into white fears that slaves
would kill as many whites as possible if
given a chance. It took only 30 years after
Turner's death for the Civil War to begin.

Nelson Davis

Harriet Tubman's second husband, who met
her in Auburn, NY, and lived with her until
he died of tuberculosis.

Queen Victoria

The Queen of England who respected Harriet
Tubman's work on behalf of slaves so much
that she invited Tubman to attend the celebration
of her 50th Anniversary as Queen in 1897.
Harriet declined based on her health and age.

Robert E. Lee

The Commanding General of the Confederate forces during the Civil War. Earlier *[1859]* as a colonel he had commanded the troops which captured John Brown after his attack at Harper's Ferry.

Sam, Bess, James, Sarah and Jane

Fictional slaves created by the author to represent elements and circumstances that Harriet Tubman and her passengers faced in traveling north to freedom. Many of Harriet's true experiences on the Underground Railroad were not recorded in detail. These families are a recreation of a trip that might have been conducted by Harriet Tubman, and most of the elements did happen on one trip or another.

Sarah H. Bradford

The author of an early book on Harriet Tubman. *Scenes in the Life of Harriet Tubman* was published in 1869 to raise money to help Harriet, always fighting poverty, to live. Bradford, a white abolitionist who lived near Harriet in Auburn, NY, wrote a new version in 1886 titled: *Harriet, The Moses of her People*, also to help Harriet's finances.

Sojourner Truth
African American leader on women's rights and the abolition of slavery. She escaped slavery in 1826, and later wrote a book published by William Lloyd Garrison, *The Narrative of Sojourner Truth: A Northern Slave.* She was a friend and colleague of Harriet Tubman, although somewhat older.

Spenser
The writer of nine historic journals, including one titled: *Spenser's Story of the Constitution.* His second story, this one, is *Spenser's Story of Harriet Tubman.* He is both the narrator and writer of these books and is one of the most literate cats in history.

Thomas Garrett
Quaker abolitionist in Wilmington, DE, who assisted hundreds of slaves to escape to Philadelphia, where until 1850 and passage of the Fugitive Slave Law meant freedom— the Promised Land—for African Americans escaping from southern slavery.

Ulysses S. Grant
Commanding General of the Union forces at the end of the Civil War. Confederate General Robert E. Lee surrendered to him at Appomattox Courthouse in April 1865, a week before president Lincoln was killed.

Walter D. Plowden

An African American who worked as a scout for Harriet Tubman during the Civil War in South Carolina. Plowden, with other black scouts, led the black troops under Tubman and Col. Montgomery through the mined and dangerous Combahee River on a raid that freed more than 700 slaves.

William H. Seward

Prominent United States Senator in New York, and later Secretary of State for President Abraham Lincoln, he and his wife Frances were benefactors to Harriet Tubman throughout much of her life when she lived in Auburn.

William Lloyd Garrison

Perhaps the leading white abolitionist both before and after the Civil War. He was also a suffragist, journalist and social reformer who published the anti-slavery newspaper *The Liberator.* He introduced Harriet to Massachusetts Governor John Andrews at the start of the Civil War, who helped her serve the Union in South Carolina which led to her leading the Combahee River raid.

William Still

An African American abolitionist who worked
with the Underground Railroad in Philadelphia.
Several thousand escaping slaves came through
his office. He kept records and wrote accounts of
the lives of slaves who had passed through his
offices. His work helped many families reunite
after slavery was abolished because he recorded
where they had gone.

Terms & Definitions

Abolitionists

People, both white and African American,
who believed in and worked for the abolition
of slavery. While most lived and worked in the
north, some worked in the south and were
agents for the Underground Railroad.

Black Codes

Laws passed by states after the end of the Civil
War *[1865-1866]*. They were an effort by many
states to suppress the newly-won freedom of
African Americans.

Conductor

A person like Harriet Tubman who guided slaves
[passengers] out of slavery to freedom in the
north on the Underground Railroad.

Confederacy
The 11 states which seceded from the Union, and then fought the Civil War to maintain slavery in the south.

Manumission
When a slave owner decided to free a slave, it was called manumission. This happened for many reasons, only occasionally because the owner believed freedom for slaves was the right thing to do.

North Star
A bright star in the night sky which is easily visible and which was used by Harriet Tubman and others to show them the way north so they would not walk in circles, or return to where they started.

Overseer
A hired plantation farm manager or field boss. As a rule, they controlled their slaves by brutal and inhumane treatment.

Passenger
A term used on the Underground Railroad which described the slaves who a conductor like Harriet Tubman was guiding to freedom in the north.

Quakers
A large Christian group which vigorously opposed slavery. Many Quakers were stationmasters on the Underground Railroad, including Thomas Garrett in Wilmington, DE.

Reconstruction
The period after the end of the Civil War, intended through the passage of laws to improve the lives and status of African Americans following centuries of slavery. It met with some success but eventually white resistance and the era of Jim Crow reversed many positive steps.

Second South Carolina
The regiment of black soldiers which were led by Col. James Montgomery, who joined with Harriet Tubman to free more than 700 slaves on a raid up the Combahee River.

Segregation/Integration
The separation of the races [segregation] or the mixing together of African Americans and whites [integration]. Over the years since the Civil War and the setting free of slaves segregation has been an important and still unresolved social issue.

Slave
A human being who is 'owned' by another person. While slavery has existed for centuries, and still does today in some places in the world, the most glaring and brutal example of slavery of African Americans existed in the United States in the years leading up to the Civil War.

Stationmaster
A term used on the Underground Railroad for people who offered conductors and their passengers a safe place to stay on their journey north, and who often transported them to their next safe house.

Suffrage
The right to vote in public elections.
African American men gained the right to vote with passage of the 13th Amendment in 1865, while women like Harriet Tubman could not vote until 1920 with passage of the 19th Amendment.

The Promised Land
For escaping slaves, a place and land of safety and freedom. Sung about in Negro spirituals, during the time of the Underground Railroad it first meant Philadelphia and other places which outlawed slavery, and later was changed to Canada where slavery remained illegal after passage of the Fugitive Slave Laws.

Underground Railroad *[UGRR]*
The process by which slaves were transported from slavery to freedom. Harriet Tubman was a conductor on this symbolic and secret railroad made up of places and people. She guided slaves from the slave state of Maryland to freedom in Canada.

Union
The states which remained loyal to the United States and did not secede and join the Confederacy.

USCT
An acronym used during the Civil War for 'United States Colored Troops.'

54th Massachusetts regiment
A regiment of African Americans which lost many men killed and injured when it joined other African American units in an attack on Charleston, SC. Harriet Tubman worked as a nurse during this battle.

Events & Places

Auburn
The small town in New York where Harriet Tubman lived after she escaped from slavery with her family and several boarders. After her death on March 10, 1913, she was buried here at Fort Hill Cemetary.

Amendment: 13
This amendment to the United States Constitution abolished slavery and involuntary servitude. It was ratified in December 1865, the year the Civil War ended. It was the first of three Reconstruction amendments which were passed to provide rights to African Americans after the Civil War ended.

Amendment: 14
This Constitutional Amendment was adopted in 1868 and has had a significant effect on interpreting and protecting Due Process and Equal Protection under law. It overruled the Dred Scott Supreme Court decision *[1857]* which had prohibited citizenship to slaves or their descendants. This was the second Reconstruction amendment.

Amendment: 15
This amendment was ratified in February 1870 and prohibited federal or state governments

from denying citizens the right to vote based on 'race, color or previous condition of servitude.' It was the last of the Reconstruction amendments.

Amendment: 19
Passed 50 years after the end of slavery and the passage of the race-related Reconstruction amendments that gave African American men the right to vote, the 19th amendment in 1920 gave women the right to vote. Harriet Tubman and other suffragists worked tirelessly to win passage of an amendment that would give women the vote. It was finally passed seven years after Tubman's death.

Bucktown Store
The small store near the Brodess farm where Harriet Tubman was a slave and the place where she was badly injured by a heavy weight thrown by an overseer at an escaping slave. Tubman suffered all her life from the head injuries she received. The store still stands today.

Cambridge, MD
The nearest city in Dorchester County to Harriet Tubman's birthplace and captivity.
[See Harriet Tubman Museum and Harriet Tubman Underground Railroad National Park].

Canada

The 'Promised Land' after passage of the Fugitive Slave Law in 1850 made living anywhere in any state unsafe for escaped slaves. Harriet conducted nearly all her passengers to St. Catharine's in Canada.

Civil War

The four-year battle between the Union *[north]* and the Confederacy *[south]* over the status and future of slavery. With the Union victory in 1865 slavery finally ended.

Combahee River raid

A Civil War raid jointly led by Harriet Tubman, likely the only fighting in the Civil War led by an African American woman. It resulted in freedom for more than 700 slaves.

Department of the South

An area, mostly in South Carolina near Beaufort, but also in Georgia and Florida, where Union forces defended a large territory entirely surrounded by the Confederacy. Harriet Tubman served as a nurse, scout and on one occasion a military leader in this unique and important outpost.

Dorchester County, MD

The county on the Eastern Shore of Maryland where Harriet Tubman and her family were slaves. After escaping slavery in 1849, Tubman returned several times over many years to conduct much of her family to safety in Canada.

Dred Scott decision
The decision in 1857 by the U.S. Supreme Court that Dred Scott, a slave who sued for his and his family's freedom, was not entitled to be free because it would deprive his owner of his legal property. The decision, which said that no African American could be a U. S. citizen, served to inflame public sentiment in the north against slavery, and played a role in events that soon led to the Civil War.

Emancipation Proclamation
Drafted by President Abraham Lincoln, this executive order freed all the slaves still in bondage in the south in 11 states which seceded from the Union. It went into effect on January 1, 1863, and under law set free three million African Americans.

Fortress Monroe
The Union fort in Hampton, VA, where black soldiers were dying at more than two and a half times the rate of white soldiers. While Harriet Tubman asked the U.S. government to help, nothing was done, which led her to return to her family in New York.

Fort Sumter

The Union fort on an island in Charleston, SC, harbor which was attacked in 1861 by Confederate guns and troops to start the Civil War.

Fugitive Slave Act

The law passed in 1850 that denied slaves any safe haven in any state in the Union. Any slave captured within U.S. borders could be returned to their owner in the south. It forced conductors on the Underground Railroad to take their slave passengers further north into Canada.

Harper's Ferry raid

In 1859, only a little more than a year before the outbreak of the Civil War, John Brown and a few men attacked the armory in Harper's Ferry in an effort to capture weapons for a slave uprising. The raid failed and Brown was executed.

Harriet Tubman Museum in Cambridge, MD in Dorchester County, MD.

Visitors are invited to stop by and learn about Harriet Tubman, her birthplace and her work on the Underground Railroad. There is a short video about Tubman's life as well. For more information contact: (410) 228-0401; htorganization.blogspot.com; or at 424 Race Street, Cambridge, MD 21613.

Harriet Tubman Home Museum
in Auburn, NY

The Harriet Tubman home is located in Auburn, NY, and offers discussions of her life, as well as other information. A visitor center is located near Tubman's longtime home. For information contact: (315) 252-2081; http://harriethouse.org/; or 180 South Street, Auburn, NY 13021.

Harriet Tubman Underground Railroad
National Park, Dorchester County, MD

The National Park honoring Harriet Tubman and the Underground Railroad opened on March 10, 2017. Located near the childhood sites of Harriet Tubman, it has a large visitor center, and offers tours. For more information: call 410-221-2290; or check their website at www.nps.gov/hatu.

Liberia

A nation on the west coast of Africa colonized by former American slaves. It was established in 1847 and recognized by the Union in 1862. Many former slaves opposed a return to Africa believing instead that they had a right to live free in their own native land.

National Museum of African
American History and Culture

A new Smithsonian museum in Washington, DC, dedicated to preserving the history of

African Americans. It opened at a location near to the Washington Monument in 2016. Find the website at: https://nmaahc.si.

Philadelphia, PA
Up until 1850 and the passage of the Fugitive Slave Act it was the "Promised Land" for slaves who escaped from plantations and farms in the south. Freedom for slaves after this time meant Canada, which had outlawed slavery decades before.

St. Catharine's, Canada
Small city which served as one of the gateways to the Promised Land of Canada. It was a short distance across the river from Niagara Falls, and was located on Lake Ontario.

Uncle Tom's Cabin
Book written in 1852 by abolitionist Harriet Beecher Stowe that exposed to large numbers of white northerners the utter brutality of slavery.

Enjoy a complimentary chapter from

Spenser's Story
ᵒᶠₜₕₑ Constitution

I Meet with Ben Franklin

Nº 1

The winter of 1787 was particularly cold. Bitter winds swirled up Chestnut Street from the river nearby, and ice and blown snow made gazing from my bedroom window nearly impossible.

It was February in Philadelphia and I was preparing to join my old friend Ben Franklin for dinner. Earlier that day I had received by messenger Ben's short note.

Franklin

"Spenser," he wrote, "will you join me tonight for a warm drink. I have learned today that our work with the 13 states is not yet finished. Please join me at eight o'clock."

As Ben lived only a few blocks away I was not overly concerned with the ill-weather. I would not need my carriage; I could walk to Ben's house. Nor was it required that I get all dressed up; Ben was not noted for his fancy clothes. In fact, he no longer wore a wig and never powdered his hair.

While I generally agreed with him on most matters, I was known to cut a dashing figure and took more care of my attire than did Ben.

This particular evening I selected a waistcoat with a high, stand-up collar with silver buttons at the sleeves and pockets. My breeches were high-waisted and long over the knees. The vertical-striped stockings led to my much-pointed shoes with quite large, round silver buckles.

My vest, of course, was made of rich, red velvet.

Earlier in the day I had purchased at the apothecary shop a bottle of Ben's favourite gout remedy—Turlington's Balsam. The winters were particularly hard on Ben, his gout and kidney stonescausing clear discomfort and making it difficult for him to get around much.

He rarely left his home any more,
but preferred to have guests join him
by his hearth.

All this is not to say that Ben was not
active in his retirement years. Although he
was now 81 years old, he served as Governor
of Pennsylvania, and also was supervising
a three-story addition to his house. He was
President of the American Philosophical
Society, was helping his grandson build a
print shop and he managed two properties
on High Street.

Dr. Benjamin Franklin was, quite simply,
one of the most respected men in all the
states. For Ben to have proposed a meeting
on such short notice meant that he had
something important to discuss with me.
I should not be late.

The walk from the State House on
Chestnut Street where I lived to Ben's home
off High Street* was only about three blocks.
I arrived at Ben's punctually at eight o'clock
and was met at the door by his charming
daughter Sally.

"Welcome to our home, Spenser,
on this bitter, cold night. I trust you had no
misstep on your walk over, and that your

family is well," she said. "Please do come in out of the cold."

"We are all quite well, thank you Sally," I replied, stepping into the warm, candle-lit foyer.

"Father," she said, "received a letter from Mr. Hamilton in New York this morning. After writing to you he has been in his study ever since. I'm sure it's a matter of great urgency."

She took my walking stick, helped me off with my heavy overcoat and escorted me down the center hall to Ben's study.

The scene on entering was a familiar one. Ben was seated behind his oak desk, peering intently at a large, wrinkled map spread out before him. All the four walls, save before two windows and a fireplace, were covered floor to ceiling with books.

Other books and papers lay everywhere around the room.

In one corner, on a round table, lay a fireman's helmet, haphazardly surrounded by still more books and papers. Drawings of the proposed addition to his house were pinned to the framework around one of the windows. A walking stick served as a paperweight for one side of his map, while a checkerboard held the other half in place.

"Good evening, Ben," I said.

He seemed not to hear, and his head and large shoulders remained bent over the map.

"It is good to see you, Ben," I said, somewhat louder.

"The problem rests with the states," he said, still looking at his map. "Always has."

He finally lifted his head and looked directly at me. "Forgive me old friend," he apologized, "I should welcome you before I discuss business."

As I've mentioned, Ben wore no wig. Instead he let his long, greying hair fall nearly to his shoulders. A large, round man he wore a brown jacket and tight-fitting vest, with short ruffles at the neck and cuffs. His clear grey eyes smiled at me from beneath his bifocals.

"I have brought you," I said, "a new bottle of Turlington's for your gout. It appears, however, that you are in fine health."

Ben had left his chair and had moved from behind his desk to greet me. Once the formalities were over, and we were both seated, he got right to business.

"I have heard from Alexander Hamilton," he said, "that the Continental Congress in New York has issued a call for a special Convention to revise the Articles of Confederation. It is an opportunity, Spenser, that we cannot afford to miss. If our nation is to grow strong we must act now to unify the states. We cannot survive if we remain 13 quarrelling, selfish and independent states."

His words took me back several years to when I was a young cat just beginning a job as caretaker at the State House. At the time—on July 4, 1776 to be exact—the colonies declared their independence from Great Britain and the taxing rule of King George III.

It was Thomas Jefferson of Virginia who had written this Declaration of Independence. Fifty-five patriots from the 13 colonies had signed it. It was the official declaration of war with Great Britain, and it had been written and signed at my State House. In fact, it was during these deliberations that I had first met Ben Franklin. Despite my youth, being barely older than a kitten, I had been able to assist Mr. Jefferson with some matters of wording. Ben had heard of my help, and we have remained close friends ever since.

The Declaration of Independence, as you will remember, led to the great War of Independence, the Revolutionary War some called it. The War lasted seven years. It was a long, hard and bloody affair, and we all lost many dear friends and family. But, at its end we had finally won our liberty and the states' freedom from foreign tyranny.

When it was over our soldiers were tired and poor, many had been away from their families, homes and farms for several years. They had won their freedom, but they had sacrificed dearly to do so. After the War they returned to their homes in Massachusetts and Connecticut, Virginia and Georgia, Pennsylvania and North Carolina. They were ready to return to their families and get back to work.

They left the political leaders in the states to form a new government to take the place of the despised British King. But because the King had been a selfish and unfair ruler, these new leaders of a new country did not want another King. They did not want a strong government telling them what to do. They did not want most of their money taken from them in taxes. So when they created the new government they made it weak and powerless. They did not let it tax the people. Without any money the new government could not do much.

While this seemed a good idea at the time, it didn't work for very long. By 1787, just a few years after the War, the states were hopelessly arguing and squabbling with each other.

The farmers who had fought in the War were still very poor and many had lost their farms. The state leaders did nothing to help. They no longer worked together, as they did during the War, and each state went in its own direction with its own government. The Continental Congress, which was supposed to be the government of all the states, was too weak and poor to do anything.

Something had to be done or soon the United States would split apart. Instead of one strong country there would be 13 weak, little countries. Many leaders, some in almost every state, did not want this to happen.

Ben Franklin was one of these men who wanted one country, not 13. His voice now startled me out of my thoughts.

"Spenser, are you okay?" he asked. "You seem not to be listening to me at all."

"Quite to the contrary," I replied, "I have heard everything you've had to say— for years now."

"I see," he said, smiling at me.

"Well, the Federal Convention will be held at the State House and will begin on May 14.

That does not leave you very much time to prepare. I expect that we will see again many old friends.

Mr. Hamilton hopes to come from New York, and General Washington should attend from Virginia with that bright young man James Madison. It should make for an interesting summer here."

I could not tell Ben that I had not heard much of what he said. But I had heard enough to know that in the spring, less than three months away, a Grand Convention would be held at my State House. And I knew that on the results of this meeting would rest the future of our beloved country—for better or for worse.

Spenser's Story of the Constitution

About the Author

After a career in journalism, communications and public relations, where he specialized in crisis communications, Paul has turned to his other love in life - writing stories for children. A writer for more than 30 years, he now has established Ozymandias Publishing Co. to serve as a vehicle for his books. Like so many talented [modestly he said] writers for children, Paul learned that publishing opportunities for new, heretofore-unpublished writers are in short supply and occur only after usually lengthy searches for either an agent or publisher.

And so, after consulting with his handsome but anxiety-riddled cat Ozymandias, they decided to undertake publishing as well as writing their own books. Fortunately for the enterprise Paul recently discovered a series of long-lost journals in a trunk written by the cat Spenser. The first of these journals—*Spenser's Story of the Constitution*—was compiled and edited by Paul and published in August 2016. This journal was particularly appropriate given that Paul spent three years (1986-89) as Director of Federal, State & Local Programs for the U.S. Commission on the Bicentennial of the Constitution, a bipartisan federal commission established by the President and the Congress to commemorate the 200th Anniversary of the writing and signing of the Constitution.

The second journal by Spenser—*Spenser's Story of Harriet Tubman*—is now available. In addition, Paul has written a number of stories for younger children (4-7)—*Stories from Squirrel Hill*—designed for reading to younger children, which will be out soon.